★ GREAT SPORTS TEAMS ★

THE GREEN BAY

PACKERS

FOOTBALL TEAM

Arlene Bourgeois Molzahn

Enslow Publishers, Inc.
40 Industrial Road   PO Box 38
Box 398   Aldershot
Berkeley Heights, NJ 07922   Hants GU12 6BP
USA   UK
http://www.enslow.com

Dedication

To Ken, an avid fan of the Green Bay Packers.

Library of Congress Cataloging-in-Publication Data

Molzahn, Arlene Bourgeois.
    The Green Bay Packers football team / Arlene Bourgeois Molzahn.
       p. cm. — (Great sports teams)
    Includes bibliographical references (p. 43) and index.
    Summary: Presents the history of the team that was started by Curly Lambeau, a meat-packing company employee from Green Bay, discussing key players, coaches, and important games.
    ISBN 0-7660-1100-3
    1. Green Bay Packers (Football team)—History—Juvenile literature.
    [1. Green Bay Packers (Football team)—History. 2. Football—History.]
    I. Title. II. Series.
    GV956.G7M65 1999
    796.332′64′0977561—dc21
                                           98-35038
                                               CIP
                                             AC

Printed in the United States of America

10 9 8 7 6 5 4 3 2 1

To Our Readers:
All Internet addresses in this book were active and appropriate when we went to press. Any comments or suggestions can be sent by email to Comments@enslow.com or to the address on the back cover.

Illustration Credits: AP/Wide World Photos.

Cover Illustration: AP/Wide World Photos.

Cover Description: Quarterback Brett Favre.

CONTENTS

*R*ay Nitschke (#66) and Herb Adderley of Green Bay pounce on the loose ball after a Don Meredith fumble.

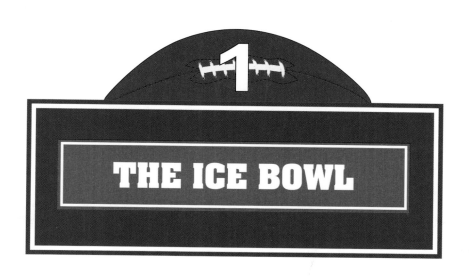

THE ICE BOWL

It was Sunday afternoon on December 31, 1967, in Green Bay, Wisconsin. The temperature was 13 degrees below zero and the wind was blowing at 15 miles per hour. The wind chill made it feel like 46 degrees below zero. But Lambeau Field, the Packers' home stadium, held a sold-out crowd of loyal fans. The winners of this game between the Green Bay Packers and the Dallas Cowboys would be the 1967 National Football League champions. That team would then play the American Football League champion Oakland Raiders in Super Bowl II.

This game started slowly. An 8-yard touchdown pass from Bart Starr to Boyd Dowler gave Green Bay an early lead. The Packers were ahead, 7–0, as the first quarter ended. In the second quarter, Dallas scored 10 points, and the Packers scored 7 more on another touchdown pass to Dowler and the extra point by kicker Don Chandler. The first half ended with the score Green Bay 14, Dallas 10.

Ice Cold

By halftime it was so cold that the officials' whistles would not work, coffee froze in spectators' cups, and the band's instruments froze. Worst of all for the players, the playing field, too, had frozen solid. Neither team scored in the third quarter as shadows began covering Lambeau Field.

Early in the fourth quarter, Dallas scored on a 50-yard pass play from Dan Reeves to Lance Rentzel. That play gave the Cowboys a 17–14 lead. Time was running out for the Packers as they started their final drive. They got the ball on their own 32-yard line with four minutes and fifty-four seconds left to play in the game.

"On the sidelines we had been discussing what to do," Bart Starr explained, "and we had decided not to try and get it back in big pieces, but just try to keep moving the ball."[1]

Time Winding Down

In the few remaining minutes, the Packers continued to move the ball toward the Dallas end zone. Now there were only sixteen seconds left to play. Green Bay was on the Dallas 1-yard line. Bart Starr called Green Bay's last time out to talk over strategy with Coach Vince Lombardi. It was third down. They could kick a field goal to tie the game and go into overtime. If they ran the ball and failed to score, there probably would

The Green Bay Packers Football Team

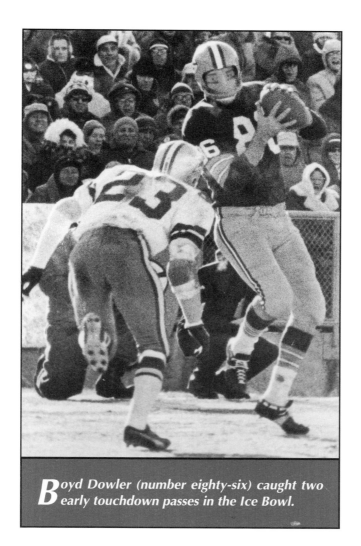

***B**oyd Dowler (number eighty-six) caught two early touchdown passes in the Ice Bowl.*

not be enough time left to kick a field goal. They decided to call a wedge play in which the fullback would carry the ball.

"I called the wedge play but I didn't tell anyone that I wasn't going to give up the ball. I felt I would have better footing. . . . And I sneaked it in there," Starr explained.[2]

When asked who decided to run that play, Starr said, "It was Coach Lombardi's decision all the way. We never considered a field goal."[3]

A tremendous roar erupted from Lambeau Field as thousands of freezing fans saw their all-pro quarterback follow his blockers across the Dallas goal line. This play has been labeled the most famous play in National Football League history.[4] The point after touchdown was good.

The Packers kicked off to the Cowboys with thirteen seconds left in the game. The Dallas quarterback, Don Meredith, threw two incomplete passes before the final whistle blew. The game ended with the score Green Bay 21, Dallas 17.

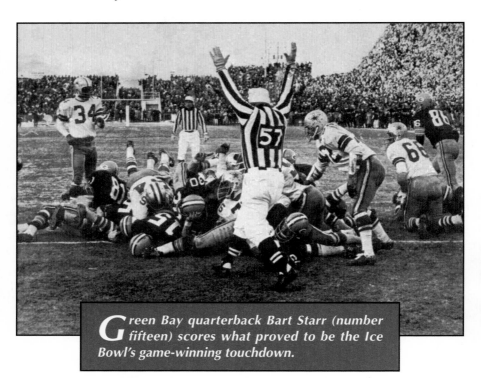

Green Bay quarterback Bart Starr (number fifteen) scores what proved to be the Ice Bowl's game-winning touchdown.

The Green Bay Packers Football Team

The Posts Come Down

Fans listening to the radio heard broadcaster Ted Moore say, "There's the gun! The football game is over. . . . The Green Bay Packers have won three straight National Football League Championships and the goal posts are coming down here at Lambeau Field."[5]

After the game, Ray Nitschke, Green Bay's all-pro linebacker, echoed the sentiments of most of the Packers' fans when he said, "The game is 60 minutes long and I knew we were going to win somehow."[6]

When reporters asked what it had taken to win the game, Coach Lombardi said, "It took all of our experience, all of our poise."[7]

This game will forever be remembered as the Ice Bowl and has been voted by many as the greatest game in NFL history. Two weeks later, the Packers won Super Bowl II, beating the Oakland Raiders, 33–14.

*D*on Hutson played for the Packers from 1936 to 1945. At the time of his retirement he was the all-time leader in touchdown receptions.

IN THE BEGINNING

The city of Green Bay has had a football team since 1893. At first, games were played with teams from nearby cities. A new team was reorganized every summer.

On August 11, 1919, a group of young athletes met with Earl L. "Curly" Lambeau and George Calhoun. During that meeting in the editorial room of the *Green Bay Press-Gazette*, the first professional Green Bay football team was organized. That was the incredibly humble beginning of the Green Bay Packers of today.

The Indian Packing Company

Curly Lambeau worked for the Indian Packing Company, a meat-packing company in Green Bay. Lambeau convinced the company to donate money for the jerseys and equipment the team needed. Because the packing company's name was on the jerseys, the team soon became known as the Packers.

Curly Lambeau had played fullback for one season for Knute Rockne at Notre Dame University. Because of his football experience, Lambeau was elected captain and coach of the new team.

"We just wanted to play for the love of football," Lambeau recalled. "We agreed to split any money we got and each man was to pay his own doctor bills."[1]

The team played their home games at Hagemeister Park in Green Bay. There were no bleachers, ushers, cheerleaders, or bands. Fans who came to watch the games sat on the grass along the sidelines. Some fans stood on the sidelines and followed as the game progressed up and down the field. There was no admission charge. A hat was passed for "free-will offerings" at halftime. There were no locker rooms for the players. At halftime, the teams went to opposite end zones, sat on blankets, and discussed the strategy for the rest of the game. The crowd usually came on the field and surrounded the Green Bay players' circle. They freely gave suggestions on plays to call during the second half of a game. Once, a halftime suggestion from a spectator proved to be the play that won the game.

A Franchise Is Born

At the end of that first season in 1919, the money collected was divided equally, with each player receiving $16.75. In 1920, the Packers continued to play against area teams. On August 27, 1921, for fifty dollars, Curly Lambeau was granted a franchise for the Packers, in the American Professional Football

J im Taylor, running back for the Packers, breaks free for a big gain.

Association (APFA), which later became known as the National Football League.

By the end of the 1922 season, the team was more than two thousand dollars in debt. After the last game of the season, five city businessmen held a meeting. They decided to encourage the people of Green Bay and surrounding communities to buy shares of stock at five dollars a share to help rescue the team from bankruptcy.[2]

As a result, a thousand shares of stock were issued in 1923. The stock was strictly a donation to the team. A committee was established to run the franchise without pay. Thus, because of community support,

*N*ew City Stadium, now called Lambeau Field, was completed in 1957.

the fledgling team survived and remained in Green Bay.[3]

Home Sweet Home

In 1925, the city of Green Bay built a stadium for the Packers. The first game in City Stadium had a grand total of 5,389 fans in attendance. Over the years, the stadium was enlarged several times until it could hold twenty-five thousand fans.

The Packers have always had tremendous fan support. However, it is a team playing in the smallest city in the National Football League and without a rich owner. Therefore, in order to survive, stock sales had to be held again in 1933, 1950, and 1997.[4]

The people of Green Bay built New City Stadium for the 1957 season. In 1965, the stadium was renamed Lambeau Field and it is still the home of the Packers. It has a capacity of 60,790 and has been sold-out for every game since 1960. Fan support is greater than ever, and the waiting list for tickets has reached forty thousand.

*L*unging forward, Paul Hornung tries to gain some extra yardage. Hornung was known as a player who would do anything to help his team.

STAR PLAYERS

Many Hall of Fame players have worn the uniform of the Packers for the majority of their careers. These are perhaps the greatest.

Don Hutson

No player ever dominated the National Football League so thoroughly as did Don Hutson, a receiver for the Packers from 1935 to 1945.[1] He was the first to develop the concept of pass patterns. He led the league in receiving for eight seasons and in scoring for five. He practiced and played with vigor.

"For every pass I caught in a game," Hutson once said, "I caught a thousand passes in practice."[2]

Hutson is a member of the Pro Football Hall of Fame. He was named to four Pro Bowls and to the National Football League's All-50-Year Team. Later he was named to both the league's 75th Anniversary Team and the All-Time Two-Way Team. He scored 29 points in one quarter, a league record. In 1994, the Packers named the team's new indoor practice facility The Don Hutson Center in his honor.

Bart Starr

Under Coach Lombardi, Bart Starr, a seventeenth-round draft choice, soon became the first-string quarterback for the Packers. He led his teams to six Western Division titles and to five world championships. He was selected to play in the Pro Bowl four times. He guided the Packers to victories in Super Bowl I and II and was named the Most Valuable Player in both.

Teammate Fuzzy Thurston recalls, "Every time Bart stepped into the huddle, we all just assumed that something good was going to happen."[3]

Paul Hornung

After winning the Heisman Trophy in 1957, Notre Dame's Paul Hornung was taken by Green Bay with the first pick in the draft. One of the most dangerous tailbacks in the league, he won the National Football League scoring title for three consecutive years, 1959–61. In 1960, he set an all-time single-season scoring record with 176 points. He shared the league's single-game playoff scoring record of 19 points until it was broken by Ricky Watters in 1993.

In 1961, Hornung practiced the loyalty to the team that Coach Lombardi preached. Hornung was stationed at the army base in Fort Riley, Kansas. Whenever he could get a weekend pass, a friend

The Green Bay Packers Football Team

would fly Hornung to the games. Hornung would play, and the friend would then fly him back to his base.

Coach Lombardi said Hornung was "a guy who probably was neither the greatest athlete nor the greatest football player . . . but who had that special ability . . . to be the greatest of the great when the challenge was the sternest."[4] Hornung was a two-time Pro Bowl selection and is a member of the Pro Football Hall of Fame.

Reggie White

One of the loudest chants at Lambeau Field was the call of "Reg-gie, Reg-gie." This cheer was for defensive end Reggie White, one of the greatest defensive players of all time. He retired as the NFL record holder for most career sacks. White helped the Packers win Super Bowl XXXI in 1997 by sacking the opposing quarterback a record three times in the game.

An ordained minister, White, who is called the Minister of Defense, said, "I don't expect anything less than to go out and give everything I've got and try to inspire everybody else to do the same."[5]

White, a future Hall of Famer, was selected for the Pro Bowl thirteen times. He was named the NFL's Defensive Player of the Year in 1998, and retired after the season.

Brett Favre

Brett Favre, the Packers quarterback, is the only player ever honored as the league's Most Valuable Player for

*W*rapping him up tightly, Reggie White sacks Patriots quarterback Drew Bledsoe. White retired as the all-time record holder for most sacks in a career.

three consecutive years, 1995–97. Favre earned that honor by leading the Packers to three consecutive Central Division championships and two National Football Conference (NFC) Championships. After the 1996 season, he led his team to victory in Super Bowl XXXI. The following year, he led his team to Super

*I*n just a short time, Brett Favre established himself as one of the most exciting football players ever. Favre won three consecutive league MVP awards, 1995–97.

Bowl XXXII, but lost in a close contest. Favre was also the first player in history to throw for thirty or more touchdown passes a year for five straight seasons.

General Manager Ron Wolf said of Favre, "He's as exciting a player as ever graced Lambeau Field, or any other field in the National Football League."[6]

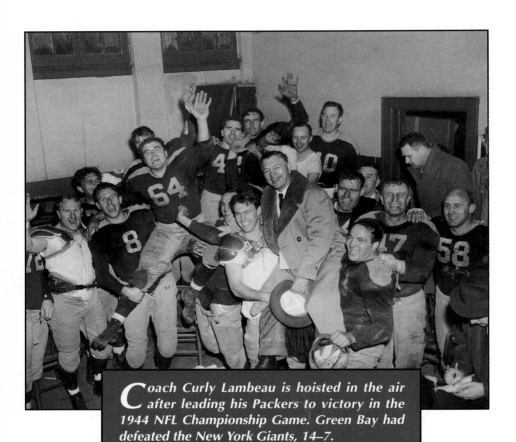

*C*oach Curly Lambeau is hoisted in the air after leading his Packers to victory in the 1944 NFL Championship Game. Green Bay had defeated the New York Giants, 14–7.

THREE WINNING COACHES

In the history of the Green Bay Packers, three men—Curly Lambeau, Vince Lombardi, and Mike Holmgren—stand out as winning coaches. Dynamic resourceful leaders in their field, they brought new innovations to the game of football.

Curly Lambeau

While he was at Notre Dame, Curly Lambeau developed an acute case of tonsillitis during the Christmas holidays and could not return for the spring semester. He never returned to school. Before the fall semester began in 1919, he helped organize the first official Green Bay football team. He became the head coach and played halfback on the team. In 1921, the team joined the APFA, which became the NFL in 1922. He played on the team from 1921 to 1929, and he coached the Packers until 1949. His teams won three consecutive NFL championships, 1929–31.

They also won championships in 1936, 1939, and 1944. Coach Lambeau's career record as head coach of the Packers is 209 wins, 104 losses, and 21 ties.

Eight players from the Lambeau years are in the Pro Football Hall of Fame in Canton, Ohio. They are Earl L. (Curly) Lambeau as a player and as a coach, and players Tony Canadeo, Arnie Herber, Clarke Hinkle, Robert (Cal) Hubbard, Don Hutson, Johnny Blood, and Mike Michalske.

Arthur Daley, a leading sportswriter for *The New York Times*, said, "Curly Lambeau was the Packers."[1]

Vince Lombardi

Altogether, in the seasons between 1949 and 1959, the Packers record was 32 wins, 74 losses, and 2 ties. In 1959, Vince Lombardi arrived and began to instill a winning spirit in his players. He said, "There is no room for second place here. There's only one place and that's first place."[2] He demanded fierce loyalty from his players. He told them, "There are three things that are important . . . your religion, your family, and the Green Bay Packers, in that order."[3]

Bart Starr said, "Lombardi was a teacher . . . he not only taught us football, but he taught us . . . the will to succeed in life, and humility to accept defeat and make something out of it."[4]

Coach Lombardi had a winning record while in Green Bay and later with the Washington Redskins. He posted 105 wins, 35 losses, and 6 ties during his career. This gives him a .740 winning percentage, the highest of any NFL coach in history at the time of his retirement.

Celebrating Green Bay's victory in Super Bowl II, Vince Lombardi is carried off the field by his players.

*M*ike Holmgren was head coach of the Packers from 1992 to 1998. He guided the team to victory in Super Bowl XXXI, its first championship in thirty years.

Lombardi's Green Bay teams never finished lower than second after 1960, becoming a showcase of football excellence. He guided his teams to five NFL championships, three of them consecutive championships, 1965–67. Under his reign, Green Bay won the first two

Super Bowls. The much sought-after Super Bowl trophy is named the Lombardi Trophy in his honor.

Lombardi is in the Hall of Fame as a coach of the Packers. Many members of his Green Bay teams—Herb Adderley, Willie Davis, Forrest Gregg, Paul Hornung, Henry Jordan, Ray Nitschke, Jim Ringo, Bart Starr, Emlen Tunnell, Jim Taylor, and Willie Wood—are also in the Hall of Fame.

Mike Holmgren

Mike Holmgren became the head coach of the Green Bay Packers in 1992. He took over a team whose record had been 4–12 in 1991. He helped his players develop to their greatest potential.

Of his first year, Holmgren said, "One of our goals was to develop a positive attitude and the idea that the glass was half full instead of half empty."[5]

His first year ended with a record of 9–7, and he was named Coach of the Year. His teams went on to win three consecutive Central Division championships, from 1995 to 1997. His teams won NFC championships in 1996 and 1997. His regular-season record with the Packers was 75 wins and 37 losses. His postseason record after the 1997 season was 8–5. The Packers won Super Bowl XXXI and reached Super Bowl XXXII. Of his 1997 team Holmgren said, "I'm proud of my guys. They're champions in my eyes."[6]

Holmgren left Green Bay after the 1998 season to become the Head Coach and General Manager of the Seattle Seahawks.

*V*ince Lombardi celebrates the fantastic finish to the 1967 NFL Championship Game. In the long history of the franchise, the Packers have had a great deal of success.

GREAT MOMENTS

n 1921, the Packers became members of the National Football League. Since then, they have won more world championships than any other team in National Football League history.

1929-31

Before 1929, the Packers had never had a losing season, but they had never won an NFL championship. In 1929, several outstanding players joined the team. One was "Iron Mike" Michalske, who could dominate any man he came up against.[1] Another new player was Cal Hubbard, a tackle for whom it often took two blockers to keep him out of a play.[2] The Packers' season ended with a record of 12–0–1, for their first NFL championship. In 1930, they repeated as NFL champions. In 1931, the Packers became the first NFL team to win three world championships in a row.

1935

In 1935, Coach Lambeau signed Don Hutson, a star player from Alabama, for $175.00 per game. When asked about playing for the Packers, Don Hutson said, "I'd never heard of the Green Bay Packers. Down in Alabama there was nothing in the papers about pro football."[3]

Hutson quickly endeared himself to the fans. In a game in Chicago against the Bears, the Bears led, 14–3, with only two and a half minutes left to play. Hutson caught a pass from Arnie Herber and ran for a touchdown. The score was now 14–10. After a Chicago turnover, Hutson again caught a pass from Herber and ran for another touchdown. The Packers emerged victorious, 17–14. Many Green Bay fans had left the stadium around the two-minute mark and returned to Green Bay believing the Packers had lost the game.

1944

In 1944, during World War II, Lambeau told reporters, "Our squad lost 10 of our 33 players to the service."[4] During that year, the undefeated Cleveland Rams visited the undefeated Green Bay Packers at City Stadium. Fortunately for the Packers, Corporal Tony Canadeo, the NFL's third 1,000-yard rusher, was home on leave. On that October afternoon, Canadeo gained 107 yards on 12 carries for the first 100-yard day in his NFL career. The Packers won, 30–21. Before returning to Fort Bliss, Texas, he was able to play in two more games to help his team on its way to a sixth world championship.

For the 1961 NFL Championship Game between the New York Giants and the Green Bay Packers, Paul Hornung was home on leave from the army. Hornung took the field that cold December day after only one week of practice. In the first quarter, neither team had been able to score. In the second quarter, with the ball on the 6-yard line, Hornung ran over right tackle and into the end zone. Later he kicked three field goals and all four extra points, giving him a total of 19

A fierce competitor, Hall of Famer Ray Nitschke was one of the most outstanding defensive players of the 1960s.

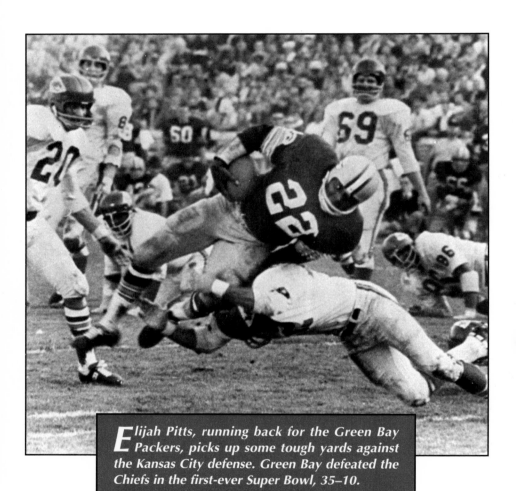

*E*lijah Pitts, running back for the Green Bay Packers, picks up some tough yards against the Kansas City defense. Green Bay defeated the Chiefs in the first-ever Super Bowl, 35–10.

points for the game. The Packers won their seventh NFL championship by a score of 37–0. Because of his record 19 points, Hornung was named the game's outstanding player, after which he had to return to the army.

1966–67

In Super Bowl I, Max McGee, an eleven-year veteran who had caught only 4 passes all season, had not been expected to play. But McGee had to replace Boyd Dowler, who was injured early in the game. Bart Starr threw a 37-yard pass to McGee. As McGee raced forward, the ball came down and bounced off his hand. He then reached back to bat the ball away to prevent an interception. But almost miraculously he was able to reel the ball into the end zone for Green Bay's first score. Later in the game, McGee juggled the ball again, but he caught it one-handed in the end zone for another score. He caught 7 passes for 138 yards and 2 touchdowns, to help make the final score Green Bay 35, Kansas City 10.

The Packers had won Super Bowl I. The following year, Green Bay repeated as Super Bowl champs. In Super Bowl II, the Packers defeated the Oakland Raiders, 33–14.

Sprinting down the sideline, Antonio Freeman hauls in his record-setting catch in Super Bowl XXXI.

6

PACKERS FOREVER

Under the leadership of President Bob Harlan, the future of the Green Bay Packers looks very promising and exciting. He hired Ron Wolf, a man with a vast knowledge of football personnel, as the general manager of the Packers. In 1997, Harlan started the latest Packers stock sale, which netted over $24 million. The money was used to finance improvements to Lambeau Field.

The Holmgren Era

When General Manager Ron Wolf arrived, he hired Mike Holmgren as the new head coach, and says of this move, "That hire was the biggest thing I've done here."[1]

Bill Walsh of the 49ers agrees. "Mike Holmgren and his entire staff have done a miraculous job in Green Bay," he said.[2]

Super Bowl XXXI

The greatest highlight of the Holmgren era was when the Green Bay Packers played the New England Patriots in Super Bowl XXXI. In that game, the Packers were trailing the Patriots by four points in the second quarter. With the ball on the Packers' 19-yard line, Brett Favre threw a pass to Antonio Freeman. Freeman caught the ball in stride. With his blazing speed, Freeman ran down the right sideline into the end zone for an 81-yard score. This 81-yard touchdown pass from Favre to Freeman set a record for the longest pass play in Super Bowl history, and the extra point gave the Packers a 17–14 lead.

Later in the third quarter, the Patriots had just battled back with a touchdown. The Packers lead was cut to 27–21, and the Patriots were still within striking distance. However, on the following play, Packers special teams star Desmond Howard took the kickoff on the 1-yard line, and, following his blockers, returned the ball for a record 99 yards into the Patriots' end zone. Besides the record for the longest return in Super Bowl history, Howard's total 224 return yards in the game also set a Super Bowl record. Because of his excellent play, Howard was the first special teams player to be named Super Bowl Most Valuable Player.[3] The Packers won Super Bowl XXXI, 35–21.

Bright Stars

The Packer Hall of Fame across from Lambeau Field helps the fans relive the many great years in their team's history. In all probability, players like Reggie

The Green Bay Packers Football Team

*D*esmond Howard's 99-yard kickoff return for a touchdown in Super Bowl XXXI broke the game open. Howard was named the game's MVP.

White and Brett Favre will be inducted into the Pro Football Hall of Fame in Canton, Ohio, as well as in the Packer Hall of Fame.[4] Their names will be added to the Wall of Fame, which overlooks the playing field at Lambeau Field, next to the other nineteen Packer Pro Football Hall of Fame members.

Other players on the Super Bowl XXXI championship team include all-pro caliber stars such as wide receiver Antonio Freeman, tight end Mark Chmura, running back Dorsey Levens, and safety LeRoy Butler. These men, as well as the other Packers, have become not only football players but also members of the Green Bay community.

Every year during training camp, approximately two hundred boys wait with their bicycles for the players to come out of the dressing room. The players ride the bicycles of proud young fans from the dressing room to the practice field, about a block away. The bike owners run alongside and carry the players' helmets. This long-established custom will continue as long as the Packers remain in Green Bay.

Ray Rhodes

When Mike Holmgren accepted the job of coach and general manager of the Seattle Seahawks, it took General Manager Ron Wolf only three days to hire Ray Rhodes as the new head coach of the Packers. Of Rhodes, Wolf said, "He brings what I believe is the most important thing available to an organization. That is a winning tradition. He has won everywhere he's been."[5]

When asked about the present Packers Rhodes said he expects to "keep this team functioning . . . and a year from now we would like to be in the big game."[6]

The Green Bay Packers Football Team

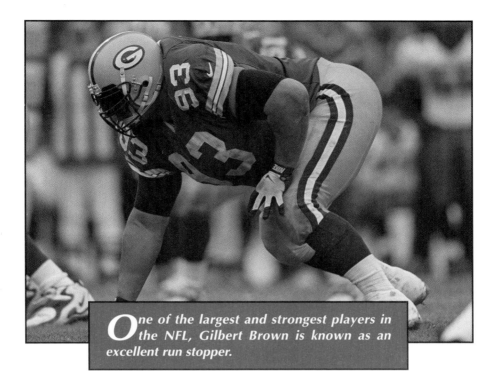

*O*ne of the largest and strongest players in the NFL, Gilbert Brown is known as an excellent run stopper.

All Green Bay fans are hoping he can accomplish that goal.

The Green Bay Fans

When the Packers play in Green Bay, the parking lot at Lambeau Field is filled with tailgaters by noon. By game time, the stadium is filled with fans chanting, "Go, Pack, go!" Packers fans come to watch their team play regardless of the weather. This ritual has been going on since 1921, and it will continue as long as the NFL exists. The Packers, the last of the NFL's town teams, will always be in Green Bay, because they are owned by the fans.

STATISTICS

Team Record

The Packers History

YEARS	LOCATION	W	L	T	PCT.	PLAYOFFS	NFL CHAMPS
1921–29	Green Bay	61	25	13	.682	—	1929
1930–39	Green Bay	86	35	4	.704	2–1	1930–31, 1936, 1939
1940–49	Green Bay	62	44	4	.582	1–1	1944
1950–59	Green Bay	39	79	2	.333	—	None
1960–69	Green Bay	96	37	5	.714	9–1	1961–62, 1965–67
1970–79	Green Bay	57	82	5	.413	0–1	None
1980–89	Green Bay	65	84	3	.438	1–1	None
1990–98	Green Bay	85	59	0	.590	8–5	1996

The Packers Today

YEAR	W	L	PCT.	COACH	DIVISION FINISH
1990	6	10	.375	Lindy Infante	2 (tie)
1991	4	12	.250	Lindy Infante	4
1992	9	7	.563	Mike Holmgren	2
1993	9	7	.563	Mike Holmgren	2 (tie)
1994	9	7	.563	Mike Holmgren	2 (tie)
1995	11	5	.688	Mike Holmgren	1
1996	13	3	.813	Mike Holmgren	1
1997	13	3	.813	Mike Holmgren	1
1998	11	5	.688	Mike Holmgren	2

W=Wins   L=Losses   T=Ties   PCT.=Percentage

The Green Bay Packers Football Team

Total History

SEASON RECORD				PLAYOFFS		
W	L	T	PCT.	W	L	NFL CHAMPIONSHIPS
551	445	36	.551	21	10	12

Coaching Records

COACH	YEARS COACHED	RECORD*	CHAMPIONSHIPS
Curly Lambeau	1921–49	209–104–21	NFL Champions 1929–31, 1936, 1939, 1944 Western Division 1938, 1941
Gene Ronzani	1950–53	14–31–1	None
Lisle Blackbourn	1954–57	17–31	None
Ray McLean**	1953, 1958	1–12–1	None
Vince Lombardi	1959–67	89–29–4	NFL Champions, 1961–62, 1965 Super Bowl Champions, 1966–67 Western Conference Champions, 1960
Phil Bengston	1968–70	20–21–1	None
Dan Devine	1971–74	25–27–4	Central Division, 1972
Bart Starr	1975–83	52–76–3	None
Forrest Gregg	1984–87	25–37–1	None
Lindy Infante	1988–91	24–40	None
Mike Holmgren	1992–1998	75–37	Central Division, 1995 Super Bowl Champions, 1996 NFC Champions, 1997

*Includes regular-season games only.
**In 1953, Hugh Devore was co-head coach with Ray McLean for two games. Their record was 0–2.

Great Packers' Career Statistics

PASSING

PLAYER	SEASONS	Y	G	ATT	COMP	YDS	TD
Brett Favre	1992–	8	113	3,757	2,318	26,803	213
*Bart Starr	1956–71	16	198	3,149	1,808	24,718	152

RUSHING

PLAYER	SEASONS	Y	G	ATT	YDS	AVG	TD
*Tony Canadeo	1941–44 1946–52	11	117	1,025	4,197	4.1	26
*Paul Hornung	1957–62 1964–66	9	104	893	3,711	4.2	50
Dorsey Levens	1994–	5	68	606	2,514	4.1	16
*Jim Taylor	1958–66	10	132	1,941	8,597	4.4	83

RECEIVING

PLAYER	SEASONS	Y	G	REC	YDS	AVG	TD
Antonio Freeman	1995–	4	54	229	3,706	16.2	36
*Don Hutson	1935–45	11	116	488	7,981	16.4	100
Sterling Sharpe	1988–94	7	112	595	8,134	13.7	65

DEFENSE

PLAYER	SEASONS	Y	G	TACK	AST	TOT	SACK	INT	FUM
*Ray Nitschke	1958–72	15	195	**	**	**	**	25	20
Reggie White	1993–98	14	216	803	322	1,125	192.5	3	20

OFFENSIVE LINE

PLAYER	SEASONS	Y	G	ACCOMPLISHMENTS
*Forrest Gregg	1956, 1958–70	15	192	8-time All-Pro selection; Selected to the NFL 75th Anniversary All-Time Team; Played in 187 consecutive games

SEASONS=Seasons with Packers
Y=Years in NFL
G=Games
ATT=Attempts
TACK=Tackles

YDS=Yards
COMP=Completions
AVG=Average
TD=Touchdowns
FUM=Fumble Recoveries

AST=Assists
TOT=Total
REC=Receptions
SACK=Sacks
INT=Interceptions

*Pro Football Hall of Fame member   **Played before accurate official records were kept

CHAPTER NOTES

Chapter 1. The Ice Bowl

1. Lee Remmel, *The Green Bay Packer 1968 Yearbook*, vol. 19 (Green Bay: Green Bay Packer Yearbook, Inc., 1968), p. 16.

2. Ibid., p. 19.

3. Ibid.

4. Steve Cameron, *The Packers* (Dallas: Taylor Publishing Company, 1993), p. 117.

5. Ed Gruver, *The Ice Bowl* (Ithaca, N.Y.: McBooks Press, 1998), p. 194.

6. Len Wagner, "I Knew Our Offense Would Come Through, Says Lionel," *The Green Bay Press-Gazette*, January 2, 1968, p. C. 1.

7. Lee Remmel, "Starr Sneak Tips Dallas 21–17 With 13 Seconds Left," *The Green Bay Press-Gazette*, January 2, 1968, p. C. 1.

Chapter 2. In the Beginning

1. Chuck Johnson, *The Green Bay Packers* (New York: Thomas Nelson & Sons, 1961), p. 43.

2. Ibid., p. 51.

3. Daniel J. Alesch, *The Green Bay Packers* (Milwaukee: The Wisconsin Policy Research Institute, Inc., 1995), p. 17.

4. John B. Torinus, *The Packer Legend: An Inside Look* (Neshkoro, Wis.: Laranmark Press, 1982), p. 19.

Chapter 3. Star Players

1. John B. Torinus, *The Packer Legend: An Inside Look* (Neshkoro, Wis.: Laranmark Press, 1982), p. 49.

2. Arthur Daley, *Pro Football's Hall of Fame* (Chicago: Quadrangle Books, 1963), p. 154.

3. Steve Cameron, *The Packers* (Dallas: Taylor Publishing Company, 1993), p. 181.

4. Torinus, p. 127.

5. Tim Mulhem, *The Green Bay Packer 1993 Yearbook* (Green Bay: Green Bay Packer Yearbook, Inc., 1993), p. 19.

6. Lee Remmel and Jeff Blumb, *Green Bay Packer 1996 Official Media Guide* (Sun Prairie, Wis.: Royale Publishing, 1996), p. 66.

Chapter 4. Three Winning Coaches

1. Arthur Daley, *Pro Football's Hall of Fame* (Chicago: Quadrangle Books, 1963), p. 233.

2. Jerry Kramer, *Instant Replay* (New York: World Publishing Company, 1968), p. 61.

3. Ibid., p. 17.

4. John B. Torinus, *The Packer Legend: An Inside Look* (Neshkoro, Wis.: Laranmark Press, 1982), p. 165.

5. Lee Remmel, *The Green Bay Packer 1993 Yearbook* (Green Bay: Green Bay Packer Yearbook, Inc., 1993), p. 6.

6. Mike Holmgren, "Coach's Corner," *Packer Report*, vol. 26, no. 12 (Sun Prairie, Wis.: America's Fans, Inc., 1998), p. 16.

Chapter 5. Great Moments

1. Larry D. Names, *The History of the Green Bay Packers, Part One* (Berlin, Wis.: Angel Press of Wisconsin, 1987), p. 165.

2. Ibid., p. 166.

3. Larry D. Names, *The History of the Green Bay Packers, Part Two* (Berlin, Wis.: Angel Press of Wisconsin, 1989), p. 79.

4. Ibid., p. 184.

Chapter 6. Packers Forever

1. Chris Havel, *The Green Bay Packer 1993 Yearbook* (Green Bay: Green Bay Packer Yearbook, Inc., 1993), p. 26.

2. Chris Havel, *Heir to the Legacy* (Louisville, Ky.: AdCraft Sporting Marketing, 1996), p. 3.

3. Chris Havel, "Rison, Howard: From Castoffs to Champions," *The Green Bay Press-Gazette*, January 27, 1997, p. B4.

4. Tom Mulhern, *The Green Bay Packer 1993 Yearbook* (Green Bay: Green Bay Packer Yearbook, Inc., 1993), p. 19.

5. Todd Korth, "Retooling, Not Rebuilding," *Packer Report*, vol. 27, no. 14 (Sun Prairie, Wisconsin: America's Fans, Inc., 1999), p. 6.

6. Todd Korth, "Rhodes' Exit in '94 Because of Daughters," *Packer Report*, vol. 27, no. 14 (Sun Prairie, Wisconsin: America's Fans, Inc., 1999), p. 8.

GLOSSARY

AFC—The American Football Conference.

free agency—An agreement between the players' association and the owners that allows players to sign with other teams when their contracts have expired.

Heisman Trophy—An award given to the best college player of the year.

Ice Bowl—The playoff game between the Green Bay Packers and the Dallas Cowboys that took place on December 31, 1967. Green Bay won, 21–17.

Most Valuable Player (MVP)—The player who is voted the most valuable in a league.

NFC—The teams in the National Football Conference.

NFL—The National Football League. Since 1970, the NFL has been made up of the teams in the AFC and the NFC.

Packer Hall of Fame—A large museum across from Lambeau Field that showcases the history of the Packers and the team's greatest players.

playoff games—Games played between the division winners and the wild-card teams at the end of the regular season to determine the world champions.

Pro Bowl—An All-Star game played after the Super Bowl. It is played by the top players from both the AFC and the NFC, who play against each other to see which conference has the better players.

Pro Football Hall of Fame—A museum in Canton, Ohio, where the greatest football players are showcased.

quarter—One of four fifteen-minute periods in a football game.

Super Bowl—The NFL Championship Game played between the winners of the AFC and the NFC.

tailgaters—People who have a cookout in the parking lot before the football game begins. Originally, they primarily cooked out of the tailgates of station wagons.

Wall of Fame—The inside wall surrounding the playing field at Lambeau Field on which is posted, in huge letters, the names of the nineteen Hall of Fame players and coaches and the years of the twelve Packers championships.

FURTHER READING

Bliss, Jonathan. *Dynasties*. Vero Beach, Fla.: The Rourke Corporation, 1992.

Barrett, Norman. *Football*. New York: Franklin Watts Inc., 1988.

Broekel, Ray. *Football*. New York: Children's Press, 1995.

Dunnahoo, Terry Janson, and Herma Silverstein. *The Pro Football Hall of Fame*. New York: Crestwood House, 1994.

Gutman, Bill. *Football*. Freeport, N.Y.: Marshall Cavendish Corporation, 1990.

Hays, Scott. *Hall of Famers*. Vero Beach, Fla.: The Rourke Corporation, 1992.

Italia, Bob. *The Green Bay Packers*. Edina, Minn.: Abdo Publishing Company, 1996.

Lace, William. *Top Ten Football Quarterbacks*. Springfield, N.J.: Enslow Publishers, Inc., 1994.

———. *Top Ten Football Rushers*. Springfield, N.J.: Enslow Publishers, Inc., 1994.

Marx, Doug. *Running Backs*. Vero Beach, Fla.: The Rourke Corporation, Inc., 1992.

Ryan, Pat. *Green Bay Packers*. Mankato, Minn.: Creative Education, 1991.

Rogers, Hal. *Super Bowls*. Vero Beach, Fla.: The Rourke Corporation, 1992.

Savage, Jeff. *Sports Great Brett Favre*. Springfield, N.J.: Enslow Publishers, Inc., 1998.

Thornley, Stew. *Top Ten Football Receivers*. Springfield, N.J.: Enslow Publishers, Inc., 1995.

Ward, Don. *Super Bowl I*. Mankato, Minn.: Creative Education, 1983.

INDEX

WHERE TO WRITE

Green Bay Packers
1265 Lombardi Avenue
Green Bay, WI 54304

WEBSITE

http://www.packers.com
http://www.nfl.com/packers
http://espn.go.com/nfl/clubhouses/gnb.html